Katharine Coman

**Outlines and References**

The French Revolution and its influence in Europe during the nineteenth

century

Katharine Coman

**Outlines and References**
*The French Revolution and its influence in Europe during the nineteenth century*

ISBN/EAN: 9783337227548

Printed in Europe, USA, Canada, Australia, Japan

Cover: Foto ©Andreas Hilbeck / pixelio.de

More available books at **www.hansebooks.com**

OUTLINES AND REFERENCES

# THE FRENCH REVOLUTION

AND ITS INFLUENCE IN

EUROPE DURING THE NINETEENTH CENTURY

KATHARINE COMAN

1893

BOSTON

FRANK WOOD, PRINTER, 352 WASHINGTON STREET

1893

HENRY MORSE STEPHENS

# TOPIC I. AGE OF LOUIS XV., 1715-1774.

## Decadence of the Monarchy.

*A.* Regency of the Duke of Orleans, 1715-'23.
    I. Financial difficulties.
       Law's Mississippi scheme.
    II. Quadruple alliance against Spain.
        *Dubois against Alberoni.*

*B.* The ministry of Fleury, 1726-'43.
    I. War of the Polish succession, 1733-'38.
      *a.* Rival claimants.
         1. Stanislas Leszczynski, supported by France and Spain.
         2. Augustus of Saxony, supported by Russia and Austria.
      *b.* Peace of Vienna, 1738.
         1. Polish throne secured to Augustus.
         2. Naples, Sicily, and Elba ceded to Spain.
         3. Lorraine and Bar ceded to France.

*C.* Reign of the King's mistresses.
       Duchess de Chateauroux, 1743-'45.
       Mme. de Pompadour, 1745-'64.
       Mme. du Barri, 1764-'74.
    I. War of the Austrian succession, 1740-'48.
      *a.* Interests at stake.
         1. The Imperial crown.
           (*a*) Francis of Tuscany, supported by England and Russia.
           (*b*) The Elector of Bavaria, supported by France.
         2. The dominions of Austria claimed by Bavaria, Spain, Saxony, Sardinia, and Prussia.
      *b.* Settlement in Peace of Aix-la-Chapelle, 1748.
         1. Francis I. recognized as Emperor.
         2. Silesia ceded to Frederick II.
    II. The Seven Years' War, 1756-'63.
      *a.* Parties.
        Austria, France, and Russia ("Alliance of the three Petticoats") against Prussia and England.
      *b.* Settlement in the Peaces of Paris and Hubertsburg, 1763.
         1. Nova Scotia, Canada, Cape Breton, and territory east of Mississippi ceded to England.
         2. Cession of Silesia to Prussia confirmed.

III. Abolition of the Order of Jesus, 1764.

References :—

   Martin : History of France. (Decline of the Monarchy.)
     I.    11–14, 26–68, Law's system of finance.
           159–166, war of the Polish succession.
           215–248, 255–260, 271, 293–295, war of the Austrian succession.
           437–440, 444–450, 470–474, 477–481, 484–505, 517–542, the Seven Years' War.
           189–198, 308–318, state of France.
     II.   179–200, abolition of the Order of Jesus.
           1–179, 295–302, 327–387, literature of the time.
   Kitchin : History of France.
     III.  389–404, war of the Polish succession.
           405–421, war of the Austrian succession.
           358–383, social and financial condition of France.
           444–462, condition of the several estates.
           463–468, Seven Years' War.
   Guizot : History of France.
     VI.  53–109, the regency.
           110–166, the ministry of Cardinal Fleury.
           167–212, the colonies.
           213–267, Seven Years' War.
           268–346, literature : Voltaire, Rousseau, etc.
   Perkin : France under the Regency.
           Chaps. X., XVII., XVIII., condition of the Court.
           Chaps. XIII., XIV., XV., Law's Mississippi scheme.
           Chap. XVI., Dubois.
   Crowe : History of France.
     IV.  156–180, the Mississippi scheme.
           201–206, war of the Polish succession.
           213–222, 226–240, 245–247, war of the Austrian succession.

# TOPIC II. CONDITION OF FRANCE ON THE EVE OF THE REVOLUTION.

A. The State.
  I. The King "reigned but did not govern."
  II. The Parliament of Paris was deposed from its functions, 1771-'74.
  III. The Assembly of Notables had not been convened since 1626.
  IV. The States-General had not been convened since 1614.
  V. The Administration was disorganized.
     a. Corruption of officials.
        Great offices were well paid sinecures.
     b. Decay of provincial institutions.
        France was governed by 37 intendants.
B. The Church.
  I. The superior clergy.
     Nonresident, wealthy, corrupt.
  II. The curés.
     Underpaid, overworked.
C. The nobility.
  I. La haute noblesse.
     Absentee landlords, wealthy, exempt from taxation.
  II. La petite noblesse.
     Resident on their estates, poor and proud.
D. The people.
  I. The peasantry.
     a. Impossible burden of taxes, exacted by the State, the Church, the feudal lords.
     b. Backward state of agriculture. Exhaustion of the soil.
     c. Depopulation of the country. Brigandage.
  II. The bourgeoisie.
     a. Enriched by speculation and trade.
     b. Jealous of the privileged orders, open to new ideas.
E. The ante-revolutionary philosophers.
  I. Montesquieu (1689-1755).
     "Esprit des Lois."
  II. Voltaire (1694-1778).
     Lettres philosophiques sur les Anglais.
  III. Rousseau (1712-1778).
     "Contrat Social."
     "Les origines de l'inegalité parmi les hommes."

IV. The encyclopædists.

Diderot, D'Alembert, Condorcet.

References :—

De Tocqueville : France before the Revolution of 1789.

149–169, condition of the people.

169–193, influence of literature and philosophy.

Rocquain : The Revolutionary Spirit preceding the French Revolution, 1–119, reign of Louis XV.

Taine : The Ancient Regime.

Bks. I. and II., state of Society.

Bks. III. and IV., revolutionary philosophy.

Bk. V., condition of the People.

Young's Travels in France : 19, 27, 45, 53, 56, 58, 97, 102–104, 125, 131, 197.

Carlyle : French Revolution, I., 1–124, death of Louis XV. and state of France.

Carlyle's Miscellanies.

II.    1–81, Voltaire.

III.   303–382, Diderot.

Hamley : Life of Voltaire.

Van Laun : History of French Literature.

III.   43–65, Voltaire.

90–111, Rousseau.

1–3, 23–25, 119–127, state of society in France.

25–36, Montesquieu.

72–83, the encyclopædists.

C. K. Adams : Democracy and Monarchy in France.

33–87, literature under Louis XV.

Louis Blanc : French Revolution of 1789.

I.   205–241, Voltaire, etc.

261–270, Montesquieu.

Smyth : Lectures on the French Revolution.   I., 43–81, Louis XV.

Morley : Rousseau.

Morley : Voltaire.

Morley : Diderot and the Encyclopædists.

## Fall of the Monarchy.

*A.* Proximate causes of the Revolution.
  I. Weakness of the government.
    *a.* Louis XVI., well meaning, but unequal to the situation.
    *b.* Marie Antoinette, "the Austrian woman," proud and obstinate.
    *c.* Court and officials, selfish and blind.
    *d.* Collapse of administrative machinery.
  II. Growing power of public opinion.
    *a.* Revolutionary literature, "the veritable paper age."
    *b.* Influence of American ideas. *Franklin, Jefferson, Lafayette, Rochambeau, Ségur.*
  III. Misery of the people, increased by dearth, drought, famine, 1780-'89.
  IV. Financial crisis. Annual deficit, 190,000,000 fr., equal to half the annual income.
    *a.* Turgot, the physiocrat (1774-'76).
      1. Abolition of monopolies.
      2. Attempt to tax the privileged orders met by storm of opposition.
    *b.* Necker, the expert banker (1776-'81).
      1. Credit not restored by business methods.
      2. Le Compte Rendu.
    *c.* Calonne, the courtier (1781-'87).
      1. Panacea, profuse expenditure and extensive loans.
      2. Proposition for general tax rejected by the Assembly of Notables.
    *d.* Lomenie de Brienne, the ecclesiastic (1787-'88).
      1. Concessions secured from Assembly of Notables.
      2. Parliament forced to register the land tax.
    *e.* Necker again (1788-'90).
      Summoning of the States-General.
*B.* Epoch of legislative reform.
  I. The States-General.
    *a.* Organization.
      1. The three estates.
        (*a*) The clergy.
          Leaders, *Talleyrand, Fouché, Gregoire.*

        (*b*) The nobles.

            Leaders, *Lafayette, de la Rochefoucauld, de Broglie.*

        (*c*) The third estate, accorded double representation.

            Leaders, *Mirabeau, Sieyès, Robespierre.*

   2. The cahiers.   Conflicting demands.

  *b*. Struggle of the Estates, May 4 to June 27, '89.

     1. The opening ceremonies.

     2. Shall the vote be by head or by order?

     3. Victory of the third estate.

        (*a*) The declaration of independence, *Sieyès*, June 17th.

        (*b*) The tennis-court oath, *Bailly*, June 20th.

        (*c*) The Royal sitting, *Mirabeau*, June 23d.

        (*d*) Final fusion of the three orders, June 27th.

            The States-General becomes the National Assembly.

II.   The insurrection of the "fourth estate."

  *a*. Causes.

     1. Distrust of the Queen and Court.

        (*a*) Concentration of troops at Paris.

        (*b*) Dismissal of Necker.

     2. Popular agitation.

        (*a*) Scarcity of work and food.

        (*b*) Orators of the Palais Royal, *Camille Desmoulins.*

        (*c*) Influence of the Duke of Orleans.

  *b*. Fall of the Bastille, July 14, '89.

    Effects of the victory of the people.

     1. On the King.

        (*a*) Recall of Necker.

        (*b*) Appointment of Bailly Mayor of Paris.

        (*c*) Appointment of **Lafayette** Commander of the
            National Guard.

     2. On the people.

        (*a*) Mob violence at Paris.

        (*b*) Insurrections in the Provinces.

     3. On the privileged orders.

        (*a*) The first emigration.

        (*b*) Sacrifices of the 4th of August.

            Privileges and exemptions abolished.

  *c*. Attack on Versailles, October 5 and 6, '89.

     1. Causes.

        (*a*) Hunger, fear, impatience at Paris.

        (*b*) Inflammatory journalism.

           *Les Actes des Apôtres, Ami du Peuple, Père Duchêne.*

        (*c*) Distrust of the Queen and Court.

           The Flanders regiment.

2. "The insurrection of women."
   (*a*) The Court and Assembly dragged to Paris. *Lafayette.*
   (*b*) The second emigration.

III. The work of reconstruction.
   *a.* The Declaration of Right, August 27, '89.
   *b.* The Constitution of '91. Fête of the Federation, July 14, '90.
      1. The King, limited powers, suspensive veto.
      2. The Assembly, one chamber, biennial elections.
         Property qualification, 3 francs taxes.
      3. Local self-government by departments, districts, and communes.
      4. Courts of justice responsible to the people. Jury trial.
   *c.* The Civil Constitution of the Clergy, July 12, '90.
   *d.* The new financial system. The assignats.

IV. Elements of difficulty.
   *a.* Radical tendencies of the people.
      The clubs.
         Jacobins, *Robespierre.*
         Cordeliers, *Danton.*
         Feuillants, *Lafayette.*
   *b.* Distrust of the King and Queen.
      1. Financial difficulties ; flight of Necker, Sept. '90.
      2. Death of Mirabeau, April 2, '91.
      3. Flight of the King, June 20, '91.
      4. Affray of the Field of Mars, July 17, '91.
   *c.* Threats of foreign intervention.
      1. Plots of the Emigrés.
      2. Declaration of Pilnitz, August 27, '91.

V. The reformed government tested.
   *a.* The Legislative Assembly, Oct. 1, '91–Sept. 21, '92.
      1. Members inexperienced. (Self-denying ordinance.)
      2. Parties.
         (*a*) The Right, Feuillants, constitutional monarchists.
               *Ramond, Barnave, Vaublanc, Dumas.*
         (*b*) The Left, Girondists, moderate republicans.
               *Roland, Buzot, Vergniaud, Condorcet.*
         (*c*) The Mountain, Jacobins, radical republicans.
               *Merlin, Chabot, Bazire, Carnot.*
   *b.* The struggle with the King.
      1. Law against Monsieur, Oct. 31, '91.
      2. Law against the Emigrés (Nov. 9) vetoed.
      3. Law against the refractory priests (Nov. 29) vetoed.

4. The Gironde ministry.
   (*a*) Declaration of war against Austria, April 20, '92.
   (*b*) Law against refractory priests (May 27th) vetoed and the ministry dismissed.
   (*c*) Decree establishing camp of 20,000 near Paris (June 8th), vetoed June 20th.
5. Insurrection of June 20th.

*c*. Breakdown of the constitution.

1. The terror.
   (*a*) The country declared in danger, July 11th.
   (*b*) Prussian declaration of war, July 25th.
   (*c*) Brunswick's manifesto, August 4th.
   (*d*) Expulsion of the Feuillants. Flight of Lafayette.
   (*e*) France invaded. Fall of Longwy and Verdun.
2. Insurrection of August 10th.
   (*a*) Assembly forced to vote
        the suspension of the King.
        the election of a national convention.
   (*b*) The Commune and the Jacobins in power.
3. The September massacres, September 2d–6th, *Danton, Marat, Desmoulins.*

References :—

Gardiner : The French Revolution, 18–117.
Mignet : History of the French Revolution, 1–190.
Morris : The French Revolution, 19–74.
Martin : History of France (Decline of the Monarchy).
    II.    279–345, Louis XVI. and Turgot.
            443–463, first ministry of Necker.
            487–496, 508–528, Calonne.
            528–534, 540–557, Brienne.
            557–597, second ministry of Necker.
Kitchin : History of France. III. 469–507.
Von Sybel : History of the French Revolution.
    I.    54–136, the Summer of 1789.
           248–287, the Economics of the Revolution.
           371–405, origin of the foreign war.
           405–531, Girondists against Feuillants.
Crowe : History of France. IV. 333–533.
Thiers : History of the French Revolution.
    I.    1–15, 81, 82, financial difficulties.
           16–46, meeting of the States-General.
           47–75, fall of the Bastille.
           76–80, 84–91, 115–118, 139–144, reform of the Constitution.

Louis Blanc : French Revolution of 1789.
    I.    270–322, Turgot.
        331–348, French court and Louis XVI.
        348–362, first ministry of Necker.
        407–419, Calonne.
        419–438, Brienne and recall of Necker.
        460–490, States-General of 1789.
        516–535, taking of the Bastille.
De Tocqueville : France before the Revolution of 1789.
        207–343, agitating influences of the reign of Louis XVI.
Rocquain : The Revolutionary Spirit preceding the French Revolution.
        120–186, from accession of Louis XVI. to meeting of the
           States-General.
Van Laun : The French Revolutionary Epoch. I. 52–248.
Smyth : Lectures on the French Revolution.
    I.    5–25, general causes.
        81–139, ministers of Louis XVI.
Quinet : La Revolution.
    I.    107–145, the States-General.
        203–272, religion.
    II.    1–31, the Girondists.
        35–103, fall of the monarchy.
Michelet : Révolution Française.  See chronological table of contents.
Mirabeau : A Life History.
Macaulay's Essays. II. 37–75, Mirabeau.
Carlyle's Miscellanies. IV. 172–254, Memoirs of Mirabeau.
Stephens : Orators of the French Revolution. I. 41–235, Mirabeau.
Yonge : Life of Marie Antoinette.
        223–240, relations between the court and the finance ministers.
        240–256, the States-General.
        257–266, 270–368, events under the National Assembly.
        369–429, events under the Legislative Assembly.
Young's Travels in France.
        153–189, 199–201, 207, 208, 211–222, 288–304, concluding
           chapter on the causes and effects of the Revolution.
Lowell : Eve of the French Revolution.
Rosenthal : America and France.

# TOPIC IV. THE REPUBLIC.

*A.* The National Convention, Sept. 21, '92–Oct. 27, '95.

  I. Parties.

    *a.* The Right, Girondists.

      *Vergniaud, Brissot, Buzot, Louvet, Pétion, Roland.*

    *b.* The Left, "The Mountain," Jacobins and Cordeliers.

      *Robespierre, Danton, Desmoulins, Marat, Egalité.*

    *c.* The Center, "The Plain."

      *Sieyès, Barère, Grégoire, Cambacéres.*

  II. Abolition of the Monarchy, September 21st.

    Trial and Execution of the King, Dec. 11, '92 to Jan. 21, '93.

  III. Efforts at Reconstruction.

    *a.* Declaration of the Republic, Sept. 21, '92.

      The Revolutionary Calendar.

    *b.* Temporary Government.

      1. The Committee of General Security, Sept. 22, '92.

      2. The Revolutionary Tribunal, March 10, '93.

      3. The Committee of Public Safety, April 7, '93.

      4. Representatives on Mission.

      5. The communes.

      6. The revolutionary committees.

    *c.* The Constitution of '93, " the most democratic ever put on paper," June 24, '93.

    *d.* The new worship.

      1. Festival of Reason, Nov. 10, '93.

      2. Festival of the Supreme Being, June 8, '94. *Robespierre.*

  IV. Struggle between the Gironde and the Mountain.

    *a.* Occasions.

      1. Question of responsibility for September massacres.

      2. Defection of Dumouriez, March 18, '93.

      3. Arrest and trial of Marat, April 13, '93.

      4. The Commission of Twelve against the Commune of Paris, May 20–31, '93.

    *b.* The insurrection of June 2, '93.

      1. Proscription of the thirty-two.

      2. Fall of the Gironde.

V. The Revolution resisted.
    *a.* France against the First Coalition.
        1. Offer of assistance to oppressed nationalities, Nov. 19, '92.
        2. War declared against England, Holland, Spain, Feb., '93.
        3. French reverses, Neerwinden, March 18 ; Mainz, July 23.
           The *Levée en masse*, August 23.
    *b.* Domestic insurrection.
        1. La Vendée, March to December, '93.
        2. The Girondist cities of the South, *Lyons, Marseilles, Bordeaux, Caen,* June and July, '93.
        3. The assassination of Marat, July 13, '93.
VI. The Reign of Terror, September, '93 to July, '94.
    *a.* "Terror, the order of the day," *Barère.*
        1. Law of the suspect, denunciations, cartes de sureté.
        2. Summary methods of the Revolutionary Tribunal.
    *b.* The guillotine at Paris.
        1. Execution of the Queen, October 16th.
        2. Execution of the Girondists, October 31st.
        3. Execution of Phillipe Egalité, November 6th.
        4. Execution of Mme. Roland, November 8th.
        5. Execution of Bailly, November 10th.
    *c.* The terror in the Provinces : *Toulon, Marseilles, Arras, Orange, Nantes.*
    *d.* Military successes due to
           (*a*) Vigorous administration of government.
           (*b*) Enthusiasm of reorganized French armies. Elected officers ; *e.g., Hoche, Pichegru, Jourdan, Moreau.*
           (*c*) Lack of co-operation among allies.
        1. Acquisition of Nice and Savoy, Flanders, the left bank of the Rhine, September to November, '92.
        2. Conquest of Holland, "The Batavian Republic," February, '95.
        3. Peace on favorable terms with Prussia, April, '95 ; with Spain, July, '95.
    *e.* Struggle of parties in the Convention.
        The Robespierrists, radical republicans.
        The Dantonists, moderate republicans.
        The Hébertists, anarchists.
        1. Execution of Hébert, Chaumette, Clootz, Gobet, March 24, '94.
        2. Execution of Danton, Desmoulins, De Sechelles, April 6, '94.
        3. Fall of Robespierre, July 27, '94 (Thermidor 9). Execution of Robespierre, Saint-Just, Couthon, Henriot.

VII.   Reaction.   Struggle between the Thermidorians and the Mountain.
    *a.* Closing of the Jacobin Club.
    *b.* Restoration of the Girondists to the Convention.
    *c.* Prosecution of the terrorists ; "the white terror."
    *d.* Weakening and final abrogation of the Revolutionary Tribu-
         nal, the revolutionary committees, the Committee of Public
         Safety.
    *e.* Reactionary legislation.
       1. Repeal of the law of the maximum, the requisition laws,
           the law of the suspect.
       2. National Guard and Commune of Paris remodeled.
       3. Religion declared free.
    *f.* The Constitution of '95.
       1. The Directory.
       2. The Corps Legislatif.
          The Council of the Ancients.
          The Council of the Young.
    *g.* Summary suppression of insurrectionists.   *Bonaparte.*
       1. The conspiracy of Babeuf, May 21, '95 (1 Prairial).
       2. Protest against the law of the two-thirds, Oct. 5, '95 (13
          Vendémiaire).
    *h.* Dissolution of the Convention, Oct. 26, '95.

References :—

    Morris : The French Revolution, 75-142.
    Gardiner : Epoch of the French Revolution, 150-253.
    Mignet : History of the French Revolution, 191-312.
    Von Sybel : History of the French Revolution.
      II.    77-112, declaration of the Republic.
         260-297, trial of Louis XVI.
         3-47, 112-193, 205-260, 297-327, 426-480, the foreign war.
      III.   3-27, 159-190, the revolutionary government.
         27-54, 135-159, 190-226, 305-439, the foreign war.
         226-305, the Reign of Terror.
      IV.   3-69, fall of Robespierre.
         183-261, reaction.
    Quinet : La Révolution.
      II.    137-186, the Convention.
         341-396, religion during the terror.
         399-474, theory of the terror.
      III.   1-39, the dictatorship.
         57-94, fall of Robespierre.
         105-167, the reaction.

Thiers : History of the French Revolution.
  II.   168–241, trial of Louis XVI.
        347–399, fall of the Gironde.
  III.  215–268, 326–396, the Reign of Terror.
        396–415, 448–551, Robespierre.
  IV.   131–181, 213–253, 303–345, reaction.
Crowe : History of France.
  IV.   531–535, repulse of the Prussians at Valmy.
        559–566, France and her foreign wars.
        570–573, 594–602, war in the Provinces.
        567, 568, 584–595, fall of the Girondists.
        608, 609, assassination of Marat.
        613–616, execution of the Queen.
        629–661, Robespierre.
Fyffe : History of Modern Europe.
  I.    40–104, foreign war.
Alison : History of Europe.
  II.   1–58, French Republic to the Fall of the Girondists.
        59–118, death of Marat, Marie Antoinette, and Danton.
        119–177, 272–338, 440–623. foreign wars.
        179–272, war in La Vendée.
        339–438, Reign of Terror.
        625–686, events leading to the establishment of the Directory.
Michelet : Révolution Française.
        See chronological table of contents.
Taine : French Revolution.
  II.   209–219, Marat and Danton.
        196–234, 297–307, the Jacobins, their character and methods.
        282–290, the Girondists.
        308–358, overthrow of the Jacobins.
Carlyle : French Revolution.
  II.   179–186, the Convention.
        190–221, trial and execution of the King.
        241–252, 299–302, organized tyranny.  *Levée en masse.*
        257–271, 286–290, 306–310, fall of the Gironde.
        275–282, Charlotte Corday.
        293–295, the Revolutionary Calendar.
        303–306, execution of Marie Antoinette.
        317–324, execution of Egalité and Mme. Roland.
        362–368, execution of Danton.
        324–332, cities of the South.
        333–339, 373–377, Atheism declared to be the truth.
        380–392, fall of Robespierre.
        417–428, fall of Sansculottism.

Stephens : French Revolution.

    II.    151–181, the Convention.

           207–281, the Girondists.

           281–215, the Reign of Terror.

L'Ancien Moniteur.

    XV.   157–232, condemnation of Louis Capet.

    XXI.  329–336, fall of Robespierre.

Van Laun : French Revolutionary Epoch.

    I.    249–339.

Smith : Lectures on the French Revolution.

    I.    481–496, war with Austria.

           496–515, the Girondists.

    II.   229–251, fall of the Girondists.

           251–374, Reign of Terror.

Wallon : La Terreur.

Yonge : Life of Marie Antoinette.

           430–462, trial and execution of the King and Queen.

Memoirs of De Laroche Jaquelein.   10–35, 55–76, 309–322, 345–365, 383–535. A most interesting account of the Vendéean war by an eye-witness.

Memoirs of Mme. Roland.

Stephens : Orators of the French Revolution.

    I.    243–361, Vergniaud.

    II.   158–204, Danton.

           287–421, Robespierre.

           467–506, Saint-Just.

Grönland : Ça ira !

    Danton in the French Revolution.

Burke : Reflections on the French Revolution.

Brougham : Statesmen in the time of George III.

    III.  46, Robespierre.

          64, Danton.

Dickens : Tale of Two Cities.

Victor Hugo : Ninety-Three.

Grove : Dictionary of Music and Musicians.

    II.   219–221, La Marseillaise.

*B.*  The Directorate.  Oct. 26, '95–Nov. 9, '99.

    I.  The war against Austria.

    The Italian campaigns, '96 and '97.

      *a.* Battles of Lodi, Arcola, and Rivoli.

      *b.* The occupation of Venice.

      *c.* Treaty of Campo Formio, Oct. 17, '97.

      *d.* Congress of Rastadt.

    II.  The misery of France.

       *a.* Financial straits of the government.

          Repudiation of assignats and mandats.

       *b.* Industrial distress.

          Scarcity of food, high prices.

       *c.* Social chaos.

          The law of hostages.

    III.  The coup d'état of Sept. 4, '97 (18 Fructidor).

       *a.* Elections of '97 favorable to the reaction.

       *b.* Army incensed by protest against partition of Venice.

       *c.* The government "purged" of reactionists. *Augereau.*

    IV.  The Egyptian campaign, '98 and '99.

          Battle of the Pyramids, Battle of the Nile, Siege of Acre, Battle of Aboukir.

    V.  The coup d'état of Nov. 9, '99 (18 Brumaire).

       *a.* The government purged of Jacobins. *Bonaparte.*

       *b.* Sieyès, Ducos and Bonaparte, provisional consuls.

       *c.* The constitution of '99, ratified by plebiscite, 3,000,000 to 1,567 votes.

          1. Division of authority.

          2. Indirect election.

*C.*  The consulate, Nov. 9, '99–May 18, 1804.

    I.  War against the Second Coalition, 1799–1801.

          Parties: Russia, England, Austria, Naples, Portugal, the Porte, against France.

       *a.* Italian campaign, Marengo, June 14, 1800.

       *b.* German campaign, Hohenlinden, Dec. 3, 1800.

       *c.* Results.

          Peace of Lunéville, Feb. 9, 1801.

          Peace of Amiens, March 27, 1802.

    II.  Reconstruction.

       *a.* Restoration of finances.

          1. Systematic taxation. The octroi.

          2. The Bank of France.

       *b.* Consolidation of the administration.

          Local authorities superseded by prefects.

       *c.* Reform of judicial organization.

       *d.* The Codes, civil, criminal, commercial.

       *e.* The Concordat, restoration of Roman Church.

       *f.* Repeal of laws against Emigrés.

       *g.* The Legion of Honor. The University.

       *h.* Bonaparte, Consul for life by plebiscite, 1802.

       *i.* Napoleon, Emperor of the French by plebiscite, 1804.

References :—

Morris : The French Revolution, 142–199.
Mignet : The French Revolution, 313–384.
Seeley : Napoleon the First, 1–105.
Hazlitt : Life of Napoleon.

I.     416–535 } Bonaparte in Italy.
II.     1–59   }
       149–259, Bonaparte in Egypt.
       337–389, Bonaparte as Consul.
       408–427, the Concordat.
       429–465, Marengo.
       466–477, the infernal machine.
       478–528, the Peace of Amiens.
III.     110–138, establishment of the Empire.

Lanfrey : History of Napoleon.

I.     60–253, Italian campaign.
       253–306, Egypt and Syria.
       353–423, Constitution of the Year VIII.
       423–455, events of 1800.
II.     45–129, first steps toward monarchy.
       153–173, the Concordat.
       182–192, Treaty of Amiens.

Von Sybel : History of the French Revolution.

IV.     293–329, 367–445, strife of parties in '95.

Thiers : History of the French Revolution.

IV.     310–314, Constitution of '95.
       430–479, 510–527, 532–540, 558–581, 599–617, Italian
          campaign of '96.
V.     31–85, invasion of Austria and fall of Venice.
       95–108, 137–141, 167–180, coup d'état of Feb. 4, 1797.
       194–218, settlement of Italy ; Treaty of Campio Formio.
       265–302, 443–460, Egyptian campaign.
       369–377, 401–412, 433–442, 474–509, revolution of Nov.
          9, 1799.

Thiers : History of the Consulate and the Empire.

I.     3–65, Constitution of the Year VIII.
       65–128, internal government.
       197–272, Marengo.
II.     121–168, Hohenlinden.
III.     117–170, the Concordat.
       241–328, Consulate for life.

Alison : History of Europe.

III.     23–122, 242–321, campaign in Italy.

379-496, campaign in Egypt.

322-378, internal government of France under the Directory.

645-697, Napoleon becomes First Consul.

IV. 249-362, Marengo.

363-452, Hohenlinden and Peace of Lunéville.

644-745, reconstruction of society in Europe.

Fyffe : Modern Europe.

I. 104-257, foreign wars.

Michelet : Histoire du XIX<sup>e</sup> Siècle jusqu'au 18 Brumaire.

123-231, the difficulties of the Directory.

231-329, the Egyptian campaign.

329-372, fall of the Directory.

Sorel : L'Europe et la révolution française.

283-336, the external policy of France.

337-358, England.

360-367, Holland.

369-379, Spain.

382-398, Italy.

399-437, Germany.

439-461, Austria.

463-499, Prussia.

Adams : Democracy and Monarchy in France. 137-215, rise of Napoleonism.

Taine : Modern Régime, Vol. I., Bk. I.

Memoirs of Talleyrand, Vol. I., Part III.

Abbott : Confidential Letters of Napoleon and Josephine.

Schlabrendorf : Bonaparte and the French People.

TOPIC V.  THE EMPIRE, May 18, 1804–April 11, 1814.

I.   The transformation.
    *a*. Assumption of imperial titles, forms, etc.
    *b*. Creation of a new noblesse.
    *c*. Conversion of subject republics into the kingdoms of Italy,
        Naples, Holland.
    *d*. Annexation of Genoa, Flanders.

II.  War against the Third Coalition, 1805.
    Parties : England, Russia, Austria, and Sweden against France,
        Spain, and the South German States.
    *a*. Failure of invasion of England.
        Battle of Trafalgar, October 21st.
    *b*. Successes in Austria.
        1. Capitulation of Ulm, October 17th.
        2. Battle of Austerlitz, December 2d.
    *c*. Results.
        1. Peace of Pressburg.
        2. The Confederation of the Rhine.
        3. Extinction of the Holy Roman Empire, Aug. 6, 1806.

III. War against the Fourth Coalition, 1806–7.
    Parties : Prussia and Russia.
    *a*. Battles of Jena and Auerstadt, Oct. 14, 1806.
    *b*. Battles of Eylau, Feb. 7 and 8, 1807 ; Friedland, June 14 ,1807.
    *c*. Results.
        1. Ruin of Prussia.  Tilsit, July 7, 1807.
        2. Alliance with Russia.  Tilsit and Erfurt, Sept. 1808.
        3. The Continental System.
        4. The Kingdom of Westphalia.

IV.  The Peninsular War, 1808–14.
    *a*. Forced abdication of the Spanish King.
    *b*. Popular insurrections aided by England.
    *c*. Battles of Talavera, July 28, 1809, Salamanca, July 22, 1812 ;
        Vittoria, June 21, 1813.
    *d*. Restoration of Ferdinand VII.

V.   The Franco-Austrian War, 1809.
    *a*. Battles of Aspern and Essling, May 21 and 22, 1809 ; Wagram,
        July 5 and 6, 1809.
    *b*. Peace of Schönbrunn (Vienna), Oct. 14, 1809.
        Marriage with Marie Louise, Archduchess of Austria.

VI.   Enforcement of the continental blockade against England.
    *a*. Annexation of Holland and Oldenburg.
    *b*. War on neutral commerce.

VII.   Franco-Russian War, 1812. ·
    France, Italy, Germany against Russia, Sweden, England.
    *a*. Causes.
        1. The Austrian marriage.
        2. The Continental System.
        3. The Polish question.
    *b*. The invasion of Russia.
        1. Battle of Borodino, September 7th.
        2. Occupation of Moscow, September 14th.
    *c*. The retreat.
        Passage of the Beresina, November 26–28.

VIII.   The War of Liberation, 1813-'14.
    *a*. Insurrection of Prussia. *Stein*.
    *b*. Alliance between Russia and Prussia. Treaty of Kalish.
        Battles of Lutzen, May 2d ; Bautzen, May 21st.
    *c*. Accession of England, June 15th.
    *d*. Accession of Austria, August 12th.
        Battle of Dresden, August 27th and 29th.
    *e*. Accession of Bavaria, October 8th.
        Battle of Leipsic, October 16th, 18th, 19th.
    *f*. Dissolution of the Kingdom of Westphalia and the Confederation of the Rhine, October.
    *g*. Insurrection of Holland, November 15th.
    *h*. Accession of Denmark, January 14th.
    *i*. Invasion of France, December 21st.
    *j*. Allied armies enter Paris, March 31, '14.
        1. Abdication of Napoleon, April 11th.
        2. Restoration of the Bourbons.
        3. Peace of Paris, May 30th.
    *k*. The Congress of Vienna, Sept. 1814–June 1815.

IX.   The Hundred Days, March 13–June 22, 1815.
    *a*. Return of Napoleon welcomed by the French, March 1st. L'Acte Additionel.
    *b*. Renewed alliance of the Powers, March 25th.
    *c*. Battles, Ligny, Quatre-Bras and Waterloo, June 16th and 18th.
    *d*. The second abdication and exile.
    *e*. The second Peace of Paris, November 20th.

*C.* The Congress of Vienna,
> *Talleyrand, Metternich, Castlereagh.*

  I.  Restoration of the old order.
- *a.* The Bourbons to France, Spain, Naples.
- *b.* The House of Orange to the Netherlands.
- *c.* The former princes to the Italian States.

  II.  Territorial indemnifications.
- *a.* Austria received Lombardy, Venice, the Illyrian provinces, Salzburg, the Tyrol, Galicia.
- *b.* Prussia received Posen, Swedish Pomerania, Rugen, Danzig, Westphalia, the Rhine provinces, the greater part of Saxony.
- *c.* Russia received the greater part of the grand duchy of Warsaw.
- *d.* England received Malta, Heligoland, protectorate over the Ionian Islands.
- *e.* To Sweden was assigned Norway.
- *f.* To Denmark was assigned Lauenburg.

  III.  Partition of Poland, Saxony, and the lesser German states.

*D.* The Holy Alliance.

  I.  Parties: Alexander I., Frederick William III., Francis I., Louis XVIII., Ferdinand VII., Naples and Sardinia.

  II.  Influence.
- *a.* Congress of Aix-la-Chapelle, 1818, against liberal movement in Germany.
- *b.* Congresses of Troppau, '20, and Laybach, '21, against insurrections in Italy and Spain.
- *c.* Congress of Verona, '22, against the Spanish revolution.

  III.  Failure, due to the death of Alexander I., '25.
> The Greek Revolution (1827) and the Belgian Revolution (1830) were protected by the Powers.

References :—

Morris : The French Revolution, 205–275.

Mignet : History of the French Revolution, 384–410.

Seeley : Napoleon the First, 116–224.

Alison : History of Europe.
- V.  245–380, War of the Third Coalition.
  - 382–529, Austerlitz.
  - 721–822, Jena.
- VI.  199–321, Friedland and Tilsit.
  - 503–611, causes of the Peninsular War.
- VII.  599–621, dethronement of the Pope.
- VIII.  726–834, retreat from Moscow.
- X.  1–79, Europe in arms against Napoleon.
  - 769–987, Congress of Vienna and the Hundred Days.

Crowe : History of France.
- V.    116-124, War of the Third Coalition.
       125-147, War of the Fourth Coalition.
       148, 149, Napoleon and the Pope.
       152-155, Peninsular War.
       160-168, Franco-Austrian War.
       183-193, Franco-Russian War.
       194-231, War of the Fifth Coalition.
       233-255, events to second abdication of Napoleon.

Van Laun : French Revolutionary Epoch.
- II.    1-39, the Empire to Battle of Trafalgar.
       40-56, Napoleon's connection with Italy, Spain, Austria, an Prussia.
       57-75, Spain and Russia.
       76-106, Fifth Coalition and fall of Napoleon.

Thiers : History of the Consulate and the Empire.
- VI.    71-99, Trafalgar.
       99-199, Austerlitz.
- VII.   3-117, Jena.
       237-362, Friedland and Tilsit.
- XI.    3-80, Talavera.
- XIV.   1-193, Moscow.
- XV.    36-77, Salamanca.
       181-218, Lützen.
- XVI.   51-171, Vittoria.
       171-277, Leipsic and Hanau.
- XVII.  3-112, invasion of France.
- XVIII. 1-121, restoration of the Bourbons.
- XX.    1-167, Waterloo.
       167-297, second abdication.
       297-440, St. Helena.

Fyffe : Modern Europe.
- I.     Chapters IV., V., War of the Second Coalition.
                  VI., War of the Third Coalition.
                  VII., War of the Fourth Coalition.
                  VIII., and pp. 439-450, Peninsular War.
                  396-438, Franco-Austrian War.
                  X., Franco-Russian War.
                  XI., War of the Fifth Coalition.
- II.    Chapter I., The Hundred Days.

Lanfrey : History of Napoleon.
- III.   65-95, Trafalgar and Austerlitz.
       95-150, Treaty of Pressburg, etc.

A. The Kings.
  I. Louis XVIII., 1815–'25.
    a. The Charter.
        1. Chamber of Peers, hereditary and appointed by the king.
        2. Chamber of Deputies, indirect election; franchise, 300 francs taxes.
        3. Responsible ministry.
            *Talleyrand*, 1815.
            *Richelieu*, '15–'18.
            *Decazes*, '18–'20.
            *Richelieu*, '20–'21.
            *Villèle*, '22–'28.
    b. The Royalist reaction.
        1. "La chambre introuvable," 1815. Retaliatory legislation.
        2. Assassination of the Duke of Berry, 1820.
        3. Restoration of despotism in Spain, 1822.

  II. Charles X., 1825–'30.
    a. Ultra-royalists against Constitutionalists.
        1. Compensation to Emigrés.
        2. Restoration of Church to ancient privileges and authority.
        3. Censorship of the Press.
        4. Dissolution of the National Guard.
        5. Antagonism of ministry and deputies.
            *Villèle*, '28.
            *Martignac*, '28 and '29.
            *Polignac*, '29 and '30.
        6. The Ordinances, July 26, 1830.
            (*a*) Rigid censorship of the Press.
            (*b*) Dissolution of the new Chamber of Deputies.
            (*c*) Restriction of the franchise—300 francs land tax.
            (*d*) New elections ordered for September 28th.
    b. The Revolution of July 27th to 29th.
        1. Abdication of Charles X., August 1st.
        2. Louis Philippe elected king of the French, August 7th.
            "The Charter shall henceforth be a reality."

III. Louis Philippe, "the Bourgeois King," 1830–'48.
    *a*. Constitutional reforms.
        1. Disestablishment of the Church.
        2. Peers not hereditary, chosen from a list of notables.
        3. Franchise reduced to 200 francs taxes.
    *b*. The strife of parties.
        1. Legitimists, *Duchess of Berry, Count of Chambord.*
        2. Orleanists, *Guizot.*
        3. Progressive doctrinaires, *Thiers, Odillon, Barrot.*
        4. Bonapartists, *Louis Napoleon.*
        5. Republicans, *Lamartine.*
        6. Socialists, *Louis Blanc, Ledru-Rollin.*
    *c*. The February Revolution.
        1. Cause : popular opposition to doctrinaire ministry, *Guizot.*
        2. Occasion : rejection of the law extending the franchise.
        3. Insurrection in Paris, Feb. 22–24, '48.
        4. Abdication of Louis Philippe.

*B*. The Second Republic, Feb. 24, '48–Dec. 2, '52.
    I. The Provisional Government, February 24th–November 4th, '48.
        *a*. The National Workshops.
        Republicans against Socialists.
        *b*. The Constitutional Convention, reactionary.
        Socialist insurrection suppressed, June 23d to 26th.
    II. The Republic, Nov. 4–Dec. 2, '52.
        *a*. Presidential election.
        Louis Napoleon, 5,534,520 votes.
        Cavaignac, 1,468,302 votes.
        Ledru-Rollin, 371,431 votes.
        Lamartine, 17,914 votes.
        *b*. Louis Napoleon made President for ten years. Coup d'état confirmed by plebiscite Dec. '51.
        *c*. Napoleon III. Emperor of the French by plebiscite (Nov. 21, '52), 7,824,189 against 253,145 votes.

*C*. The Second Empire (Dec. 2, '52–Sept. 4, '70).
    I. Foundations of the Empire.
        *a*. Absolutism. The Orsini bombs.
        *b*. Magnificence.
        1. Internal improvements.
        2. Exposition of '67.
        *c*. Military glory.
        1. Part taken by France in the Crimean War, '54–'56.
        2. Part taken by France in the Austro-Sardinian War, '59.

II. The Empire was ruined by
    *a.* Administrative corruption.
    *b.* Ambition for military achievement.
       1. The Mexican expedition, '61–'67.
       2. The Franco-Prussian War, '70.
         (*a*) Catastrophe of Sedan, Sept. 2.
         (*b*) Deposition of Napoleon, Sept. 5.
         (*c*) Government of National Defense.

*D.* The Third Republic. Sept. 5, '70.
  I. The German invasion.
    *a.* The siege of Paris. *Trochu*, Sept. 19, '70–Jan. 28, '71.
    *b.* Fruitless organization of the Provinces. *Gambetta.*
    *c.* The National Assembly. *Thiers.*
    *d.* The Treaty of Paris, Feb. 28, '71.
  II. The Commune, March 18–May 29, '71.
    *a.* Insurrectionary Paris against Thiers and the National Assembly at Versailles.
    *b.* The second siege of Paris.
    *c.* The bloody suppression of the Commune.
  III. The Republican Constitution established, Feb. '75.
    *a.* Legislature (Senate and Chamber of Deputies) elected by universal suffrage.
    *b.* President elected by the National Assembly.
    *c.* Responsible ministry.
  IV. Strife of parties.
    *a.* Republicans, *Gambetta, Simon, Ferry, Freycinet.*
    *b.* Monarchists, *Count of Chambord, Count of Paris.*
    *c.* Imperialists, "*Plon-Plon,*" *Boulanger.*
    *d.* Socialists, *Ledru-Rollin, Lafargue.*

References :
Adams : Democracy and Monarchy in France, 217–473.
Lamartine : Restoration of Monarchy in France.
  I. 249–258, character of Louis XVIII.
    292–301, the Count of Artois.
    301–317, the royal family.
    423–432, 445–452, 480–492, government of Louis XVIII.
  III. 96–112, 209–213, 234–243, 252–255, 372–382, 409–412, 422–427, 439–482, reign of Louis XVIII.
Lamartine : Histoire de la Révolution de 1848.
Wright : History of France.
  III. 260–268, 292–295, 297, 298, 303–311, 323–332, 339–343, 357–362, reign of Louis XVIII.

XXIX., the war in the provinces.

XXX., fall of Paris.

Macdonell : France since the First Empire.

Simon : The Government of Thiers.   I.   357–533, the Commune.

Le Goff : Life of Thiers.

> 138–160, the Republic of 1848.
>
> 161–188, Thiers and the Empire.
>
> 203–243, Thiers' presidency.

Dréolle : La Journée du 4 Septembre.

Simon : Souviens toi du deux Decembre.   1–95, Boulanger.

Lepage : Histoire de la Commune.

Quinet : Paris.   The Franco-Prussian War.

Scribner's Magazine.

> I.   (1887).   3, 161, 289, 447, reminiscences of Siege and Commune of Paris.   Washburne.

Edinburgh Review.

> CLIX., 82, Paris in 1871.

Towle : Certain Men of Mark.

> 66–95, Gambetta.
>
> 154–182, Victor Hugo.

King : French Leaders.

> 55–75, Thiers.
>
> 75–96, Gambetta.

Simon : Thiers, Guizot, Rémusat.

Mounod's Articles on contemporary France in the Contemporary Review.   42 : 155, 641.   43 : 157.   44 : 105, 616.   45 : 424.   46 : 127.   47 : 120.   48 : 126, 887.   49 : 881.   50 : 728.   51 : 434.   52 : 428.   53 : 301, 902.   54 : 897.   55 : 477, 495.   56 : 629.

Lebon and Pelſet : France as it is.

Dilke : European Politics.   Chapter II.

# TOPIC VII. BELGIUM IN THE NINETEENTH CENTURY.

*A.* Result of the Napoleonic Wars.
   I.  Flanders annexed to France, 1792.
   II.  Flanders annexed to Holland, 1815.

*B.* The Revolution of 1830.
   I.  Cause : hostility to the Dutch Government.
   II.  Events.
      *a.* Insurrection in Brussels, August 25th.
      *b.* Declaration of Independence, November 18th.
      *c.* Independence recognized by the Powers. The London conference, Jan. 31, '31.
   III.  The new government.
      *a.* Monarch, Leopold of Saxe-Coburg.
      *b.* Legislature.
         1. Senate, property qualification,—2100 francs taxes.
         2. Chamber of Representatives.
            Franchise,—40 francs taxes, 133,000 voters.
      *c.* Responsible ministry.

*C.* Insurrection of April 18, 1893.
   I.  Universal suffrage demanded by the people.
   II.  Extension of the suffrage granted by the Legislature ; 2,000,000 votes.

References :—

    Fyffe : Modern Europe, II., 381–389.
    Dyer : Modern Europe, V., 404–409.
    The Annual Encyclopedia, 1893.

# TOPIC VIII. SPAIN IN THE NINETEENTH CENTURY.

*A.* Effect of the Napoleonic Wars.
  I. Forced abdication of Charles IV. and Ferdinand VII., 1808.
  II. Reign of Joseph Bonaparte, 1808–1813.
  III. Influence of French ideas.
   *a.* The Constitution of 1812.
   *b.* Abolition of the Inquisition.
   *c.* Confiscation of monastic property.
  IV. Struggle for national independence.

*B.* Ferdinand VII. 1814–'33.
  I. Absolutism.
   *a.* Rejection of the Constitution of 1812.
   *b.* Restoration of the order of Jesuits and the Inquisition.
   *c.* Rigid censorship of the press.
  II. Rebellion.
   *a.* The secret societies.
   *b.* Insurrection of the troops at Cadiz, *Riego*, Jan. 1, 1820.
   *c.* King forced to take oath to Constitution of 1812, March 7, '20.
    1. Abolition of the Inquisition.
    2. Freedom of the press.
   *d.* Constitutional government resisted by the Exaltados (republicans), and the Serviles (absolutists).
   *e.* The French invasion.
    Restoration of absolutism. The Reign of Terror, 1822.
  III. Struggle over the succession.
    The Pragmatic Sanction.

*C.* Isabella II. 1833–'68.
  I. The Carlist War, '33–'39.
    Christinos (liberals) against Carlists (absolutists).
  II. The constitutional struggle.
   *a.* The Royal Statute, 1834.
   *b.* Constitution of 1812 conceded, 1836.
   *c.* Constitution of 1837.
   *d.* Strife of parties.
    Conservatives, *Narvaez*, against Progressists, *Espartero*.

*D.* Revolution of '68.
  I. Isabella driven from Spain.
  II. Provisional government under Serrano and Prim.
  III. Reign of Amadeus of Savoy, '70–'73.
  IV. Federal republic attempted, '73–'75.

*E.* Reign of Alphonso XII., '74–'86.
   I. Government, constitutional monarchy.
  II. State religion, Roman Catholic, but Protestant worship tolerated.
 III. Parties, monarchists against republicans.

         *Canovas against Castelar.*

*F.* Reign of Alphonso XIII., 1886—
Regency of Maria Christina.


References :—

   Müller : Political History of Recent Times.
        42–53, reign of Ferdinand.
        56–62, Portugal.
        143–149, 405–408, reign of Isabella.
        478–482, revolutions of 1870–1874.
        599–603, reign of Alphonso XII.
   Dyer : Modern Europe.
    V.   256–276, 294–299, 340, War of Independence.
        369 and 370, Constitution of 1812.
        370–378, 423 and 424, Ferdinand VII.
        424–431, 470 and 471, Isabella.
        541 and 542, Spanish affairs to 1870.
   Abbott : Romance of Spanish History.
        402–432, exile and return of the Spanish Court.
        432–462, the Revolution.
   Fyffe : Modern Europe.
    I.   359–396, 439–451, Spain in the Napoleonic Wars.
    II.  9–12, 89, 90, 166–236, 422–442, reigns of Ferdinand VII.
        and Isabella.
   Alison : History of Europe (1815–1852).
    II.  1 and 2, 9–25, 29–36, 60–85, 567–612, 614–619, 623, 626–
        634, 641–645, 679–708, 735–738, reign of Ferdinand
        VII. to 1823.
    IV.  482–484, attempts to revolutionize Spain from Paris.
        501–504, Spanish succession in 1830.
    VII. 594–613, Spanish marriages.
   Wallis : Spanish History.
        31–43, review of history to 1845.
        44–66, Constitution of 1845.
        120–128, 140–145, 173–183, Spanish politicians.
        183–194, monarchy in Spain.
        250–255, 265–290, the church.
        377–394, prospects of Spain in 1845.

Duff: Studies in European Politics.

        5–28, reigns of Ferdinand VII. and Isabella II.

        29–64, condition of Spain in 1865.

Buckle: History of Civilization in England.

  II.    106–122, Spanish civilization in nineteenth century.

Harrison: History of Spain.

        630–653, Ferdinand VII.

        655–695, Isabella II.

        695–702, reign of Alphonso XII.

## TOPIC IX. GERMANY IN THE NINETEENTH CENTURY.

*A.* Result of the Napoleonic wars.
    I.  Territorial transformations.
        *a.* Reduction of Austria and Prussia.
        *b.* Augmentation of lesser states; *e. g.,* Bavaria, Würtemberg, Baden, Westphalia.
        *c.* Confiscation of ecclesiastical states and free cities.
    II.  Final extinction of the Holy Roman Empire.
    III.  Revival of national patriotism.
    IV.  Settlement by the Congress of Vienna.
        *a.* Austria loses German and acquires Italian and Slavic territory.
        *b.* Prussia loses Slavic and acquires German territory.
        *c.* Ecclesiastical states and free cities not restored.
        *d.* Bavaria, Würtemberg, Hanover, and Saxony retain second rank.
        *e.* The Act of Confederation, June 8, 1815.
            1. League of thirty-nine sovereign states.
            2. Federal Diet and Ministry under presidency of Austria.
            3. Constitutional government promised to the states.

*B.* Influence of the French Revolutions.
    I.  The Great Revolution.
        *a.* Doctrines embraced by students of the universities.
        *b.* Murder of Kotzebue.
            1. The Carlsbad Revolutions, 1819.
            2. The Final Act, 1820.
    II.  The Revolution of 1830.
        *a.* Insurrections in Saxony, Hesse-Cassel, Hanover, Brunswick.
        *b.* The liberal movement discredited.
    III.  The Revolution of '48.
        *a.* Insurrections at Vienna, Berlin, Munich, Dresden, Hanover, etc.
        *b.* Constitutional reforms conceded. "The March Cabinets."
        *c.* Attempt to organize a national union.
            1. The Ante-Parliament, March 30–April 4, '48.
            2. The National Assembly at Frankfort, May 18, '48–June 18, '49.
            3. Rivalry of Prussia and Austria.
                (*a*) Failure of the Prussian Union.
                (*b*) Re-establishment of the Federal Diet.

*C.* Prussian Ascendency. *Bismarck.*

   I. The Customs-union.

  II. The Schleswig-Holstein War, '64.
      The Gastein Convention.

 III. The Austro-Prussian War, June 22–July 22, '66.
    *a.* Parties. Prussia, smaller north German states, and Italy against Austria, South Germany, Saxony, and Hanover.`
    *b.* Events.
       1. Occupation of Hanover, Hesse, and Saxony by Prussian troops.
       2. Invasion of Bohemia, Battle of Königgrätz (Sadowa), July 3, '66.
       3. Defeat of the Army of the Confederation, Aschaffenburg, July 14th.
    *c.* Results. Peace of Prague, August 23d.
       1. The North German Confederation formed without Austria.
       2. Schleswig-Holstein, Hanover, Hesse, Nassau, and Frankfort annexed to Prussia.
       3. Venice ceded to Italy. Peace of Vienna, October 3d.

 IV. The Franco-Prussian War, July 19, '70–March 3, '71.
    *a.* Causes.
       1. The Luxembourg question.
       2. Hohenzollern candidate for the Spanish throne.
    *b.* Events.
       1. Invasion of France.
          (*a*) Battles of Saarbrücken, Weissenberg, Worth, Gravelotte.
          (*b*) Sieges of Metz, Strasburg.
          (*c*) Capitulation of Sedan.
          (*d*) Siege of Paris.
       2. Proclamation of the Empire, Jan. 18, '71.
    *c.* Results.
       1. Acquisition of Alsace-Lorraine.
       2. Political unity of the German nation.

  V. The Constitution of the German Empire.
    *a.* Hereditary Emperor, King of Prussia.
    *b.* Legislature.
       1. Federal Council (Bundesrath), representation of the twenty-five federated states.
       2. Imperial Parliament (Reichstag), representation of the people ; manhood suffrage.

VI.   Strife of parties.
    *a*. Conservatives.   Caprivi, Hammerstein.
    *b*. National Liberals.   Bennigsen.
    *c*. Freisinnige.   Richter, Bamberger.
    *d*. Social democrats.   Liebknecht, Bebel.

References :—

Lewis : History of Germany.
    666–688, German Confederation.
    689–711, War of 1866.
    712–747, War of 1870.
    748–773, the New German Empire.
Menzel : History of Germany.
  III.  368–383, the German Confederation.
    386–390, the German Customs-union.
    390–408, the Revolutions.
    408–416, the Struggle of the Diets.
Müller : History of Recent Times.
    1–23, struggles for a Constitution.
    159–169, internal conditions.
    212–252, revolutions.
    300–393, supremacy of Prussia.
    409–459, Franco-Prussian War.
    493–504, German Empire and the Culturkamf.
    630–652, Germany since 1876.
Alison : History of Europe (1815–1852).
  V.  1–9, Confederation of 1815.
    14–35, outbreak in 1819 and '20.
  VIII.  478–494, 500–514, 526–550, 557–571, 582, revolution of 1848.
    514–524, 583–590, Schleswig-Holstein.
    596–673, revolution of 1848 in Austria.
    674–756, Hungarian revolution.
Fyffe : History of Europe.
  II.  20–30, 63–71, 78–90, 121–153.
  III.  1–34, 114–156, 305–524.
Murdock : Reconstruction of Europe.
    Chapters 14, 15, 16, 17, 18, 19, 21, 24, 25, 26, 27.
Maurice : Revolutionary Movement of 1848 and '49.
    Chapters 1, 4, 7, 8 ; pp. 402–417.
Malet : Overthrow of the Germanic Confederation in 1866.
Von Moltke : The Franco-German War.
Biedermann : Dreizig Jahre Deutsche Geschichte.

Hottinger : Der Deutsch-Französische Krieg.

Freitschke : Deutsche Geschichte im Neunzehnten Jahrhundert.

Bryce : Holy Roman Empire. 411–445, the new German Empire.

Hudson : Louisa, Queen of Prussia.

   I.    367–416, the young Queen.

        417–438, Frederick William III.

   II.   48–52, 105–199, Prussia's foreign policy.

        201–326, war of liberation.

        330–456, Louisa's part in the regeneration of Prussia.

Bismarck in the Franco-Prussian War.

   I.    94–117, Sedan.

   II.   88–117, 159–165, 169–182, 205–209, 227–244, 278–319, 332–333, the Germans before Paris.

Strauss : Men Who Have Made the New German Empire.

   I.    1, 2, 6–32, William I., and brief review of this period.

        95-181, Bismarck and review of his work.

Autobiography of Prince Metternich.

   II.   553–585, Congress of Vienna.

   III.  189–196, 253–294, 422–431, 453–476, Metternich's German policy.

Dilke : Present Position of European Politics, 1–56.

Tuttle : German Leaders. 1–21, Bismarck and his work.

Rand : Economic History since 1763. 170–207, the customs-union.

Fortnightly Review : 1 ; 664.

The Forum : 11 (1890) ; 481, Emperor William II.

The New Review : 2 ; 289, the fall of Prince Bismarck.

Harpers' Magazine : 81 ; 75, Furst Bismarck.

Nineteenth Century : 27 ; 688, Prince Bismarck.

Westminster Review : 133 ; 333, Prince Bismarck's position.

The Nation : 50 ; 311, French Interest in Bismarck's retirement.

*A.* Effect of the Napoleonic Wars.
    I. Overthrow of the hereditary dynasties.
    II. Establishment of republics.
        Cisalpine, 1797.
        Cispadane, 1797.
        Ligurian, 1797.
        Roman, 1798.
        Parthenopean, 1799.
    III. Annexation of Venice to Austria; of Nice, Savoy, and Genoa to France.
    IV. Establishment of the kingdoms of Italy and Naples.
    V. Settlement by the Congress of Vienna.
       *a.* Venice and Lombardy assigned to Austria.
       *b.* Nice, Savoy, Piedmont restored to Sardinia, and Genoa annexed.
       *c.* Old dynasties restored in Naples, the Papal States, Tuscany, etc.
    VI. Transformation of the people.
       *a.* Inter-state barriers broken down.
       *b.* Alien dynasties discredited.
       *c.* Influence of the French Revolution.

*B.* Regeneration of Italy.
    I. Influence of the Carbonari.
       *a.* The insurrections of 1820.
       Constitutional governments conceded in Naples and Piedmont, but absolutism restored by Austrian intervention.
       *b.* The insurrections of 1830.
       Risings in Parma, Modena, and the Papal States suppressed by Austrian troops.
    II. Influence of Mazzini and Gioberti.
       *a.* Italian federation advocated by Gioberti, Charles Albert, Pius IX.
         1. Constitutional governments conceded in Naples, Sardinia, Tuscany, Rome, '48.
         2. Austrian garrisons expelled from Milan and Venice. *Daniele Manin.*
         3. Austro-Sardinian War, March, '48–July, '49.
           (*a*) Battle of Custozza, July 25, '48.
           (*b*) Salasco Armistice, Aug. 9, '48–March 20, '49.
           Neapolitan and Papal troops withdrawn.

(*c*) Battle of Novara, March 23, '49.
Abdication of Charles Albert.
Restoration of Austrian rule.
*b*. National unity and republican government advocated by Mazzini and Garibaldi.
  1. Murder of Pellegrino Rossi, Nov. 15, '48.
  2. Republican governments established in Rome, Tuscany, and Venice.
    (*a*) The Roman Republic overcome, and the Pope restored by the French troops.
    (*b*) The Venetian Republic reduced by Austrian troops.
III. The Sardinian leadership. *Victor Emmanuel, Cavour, D'Azelio.*
  *a*. Participation in the Crimean War and the Berlin Conference.
  *b*. The Austro-Italian War, '59.
    1. Parties : Sardinia and France against Austria.
    2. Battles : Magenta, June 4th ; Solferino, June 24th.
    3. Results.
      *a*. Truce of Villafranca ; Peace of Zurich.
        1. Lombardy ceded to Sardinia.
        2. Sovereigns to be restored in Tuscany, Modena, and Romagna.
        3. Italian federation under the presidency of the Pope.
      *b*. Accession of Tuscany, Parma, Modena, and Romagna. *Ricasoli.*
      *c*. Accession of Sicily, Naples, and the Papal States.
        1. The Thousand of Marsala. *Garibaldi.*
        2. Flight of Francis II. from Naples.
Siege of Gaeta, Nov., '60–Feb., '61.
        3. Invasion of the Papal States by Piedmontese troops. Battle of Castel Fidardo, Sept. 11, '60.
        4. Victor Emmanuel declared King of Italy by a National Parliament, March 18, '61.
  *d*. Acquisition of Venice, '66.
The Austro-Prussian War.
Battles of Custozza and Lissa.
  *e*. Acquisition of Rome.
    1. Garibaldi's fruitless expedition, '62.
    2. The September Convention, '64.
    3. Garibaldi's second attempt, '67.
    4. The Franco-Prussian War., '70
      (*a*) Withdrawal of the French Troops.
      (*b*) Accession of Rome by plebiscite.

*C.* Contemporary Italy.
  I. Constitution.
    *a.* Parliament.
      1. Senate, composed of royal princes and nominees.
      2. Chamber of Deputies.
        Franchise, 19 lire annual taxes.
      3. Responsible ministry.
    *b.* Local government.
      1. Provincial.
        Prefect appointed by the king; Council elected by the people.
      2. Communal.
        Syndic and Council, elected by the people in communes of more than ten thousand; appointed by the king in communes of less than ten thousand.
  II. Relation of Church and State.
    "The Catholic, Apostolic, and Roman religion is the sole religion of the State."
    *a.* The Pope is divested of temporal power, but recognized as head of the Church.
    *b.* The Church is subordinate to the State.
      1. Nominations to bishoprics, etc., must be ratified by the king.
      2. Legislation valid against protest of the Church.
        (*a*) Siccardi Laws.
        (*b*) Laws of the Papal Guarantees.
        (*c*) Suppression of the Order of Jesuits.
        (*d*) Partial suppression of religious houses.
        (*e*) The new code.
  III. Strife of parties.
    *a.* The Right (*Crispi*) maintains the Monarchy, the Papal Guarantees, the Triple Alliance.
    *b.* The Left (Radicals, Republicans, and Socialists), opposes military policy, heavy taxes, the Pope, and the clergy.
    *c.* The Left-center (Moderates) holds the balance of power.
References :—
  Müller : Political History of Present Times.
        23–42, insurrections of 1820.
        129–133, insurrections of 1830.
        202–212, revolution of 1848.
        270–291, events of 1860.
        327, 357–360, acquisition of Venetia.
        400–405, 476–478, acquisition of Rome.

Hunt: History of Italy, 221–261.

Probyn: Italy, 1815–1890.

Spalding: Italy and the Italian States.
    III.   98–110, state of Italy.
          123–131, insurrections of 1820.
          132–140, insurrections of 1830.
          197–200, 265–272, literature of the 19th Century.
          224–230, character of the Italians.

Abbott: History of Italy, 531–622.

Wrightson: History of Modern Italy.
          1–22, the patriot parties.
          51–60, revolutions of 1820 and 1830.
          224–231, opening of War of 1848.
          337–352, the Novara campaign.
          353–380, concluding events of the war.

Thayer: Dawn of Italian Independence.
    I.    Book II., III., absolutism against revolution, 1815–48.
    II.  Party struggles of 1848.

Godkin: Life of Victor Emmanuel II.
    I.    9–36, insurrections of 1820 and 1830.
          47–65, war of independence in 1848.
          178–253 $\left.\right\}$, the Austro-Italian Wars.
    II.  15–34
          35–62, revolution in Naples, 1860.
          63–72, Victor Emmanuel, King of Italy.
          111–121, acquisition of Venetia.
          84–102, 133–148, 168, 172–181, 185–192, the Roman question.

Massari: Vita di Vittorio Emanuele II.

Dicey: Victor Emmanuel II.

Alison: History of Europe (1815–1852).
    III.  91–112, insurrections of 1820.
    VII.  61–86, events of 1848.

Fyffe: Modern Europe.
    II.   178–185, 189–204, 398–405, 465–476.
    III.  14–19, 55–61, 96–113, 241–305, 361–364.

Italy and the Italians.
    I.    85–114, character of the Neapolitans.
          165–202, the Tuscans.
          262–308, the rule of Napoleon.
    II.  44–79, Kingdom of Sardinia, and insurrections of 1820.
          160–173, the Romans.
          182–206, insurrection at Naples, 1820.

Gallenga : The Pope and the King.

    I.    14–23, condition of Italy.

        48–76, revolution in Rome, 1848.

        77–110, first war of independence.

        111–114, 119–140, Victor Emmanuel II. and his work for Italy.

        141–186, the reactionary Pope.

        202–244, events of 1860.

        266, 267, 268–278, 280–290, 335–367, 371–410, events at Rome.

        259–262, acquisition of Venetia.

    II.    1–37, 176–187, 249–263, the Pope a prisoner at Rome.

Botta : Italy under Napoleon.

    I.    Chapters III., IV.

    II.    35–95, 311–354, 392–452.

Arrivabene : Italy under Victor Emmanuel II. (in 1859 and 1860).

    I.    1–8, preparation for war.

        58–80, Magenta.

        178–219, Solferino and San Martino.

        256–277, Peace of Villafranca.

        335–349, Parma and Modena.

        364–392, Papal states.

    II.    28–58, 166–262, 285–328, Garibaldi in Sicily and Naples.

        386–408, United Italy.

Autobiography of Prince Metternich.

    III.    88–107, condition of Italy in 1817.

Memoir of Count Giuseppe Pasolini.

    Chapters III.,—VIII., Pontificate of Pius IX.

Souvenirs historiques de la Marquise Constance d'Azelio—1835–1861.

D'Azelio : I miei Ricordi.

Marriott : Makers of Modern Italy.

    Mazzini, Cavour, Garibaldi.

Joseph Mazzini : Life and Writings.

New Englander :—

    38 : 487, Mazzini in the Italian revolution.

Autobiography of Garibaldi.

Berti : Diario di Cavour ; Conte di Cavour.

International Review :—

    3 : 642, How New Italy became a Nation.

    5 : 303, The New King of Italy and the New Pope.

Dilke : Present Position of European Politics.

    Chapter V.

*A.* Alexander I., 1801–1825.
    I.  Results of the Napoleonic Wars.
        *a.* Russia recognized as a predominant power,
            At Tilsit, 1807.
            At Paris, 1814.
            At Vienna, 1815.
        *b.* Annexation of Poland.
        *c.* Conversion of the Czar to reactionary policy.
            The Holy Alliance.
        *d.* Conversion of the army to ideals of the French Revolution.
            Insurrection in favor of Constantine, December, 1825.

*B.* Nicholas, "the iron Czar," 1825–1855.
    I.  The War of Grecian Independence, '21–'29.
        *a.* Joint intervention of Russia, England and France.
        *b.* Battle of Navarino, '27.
        *c.* Peace of Adrianople, '29.
            Independence of Greece secured.
    II.  Revolution in Poland, '30–'32.
        *a.* The insurgents reduced to submission.
        *b.* The Organic Statute, Feb., '32. Poland deprived of its constitution.
    III.  The Crimean War, '54–'56.
        *a.* Cause : Russia's designs on Constantinople.
        *b.* Parties : England, France, Sardinia and Turkey, against Russia.
        *c.* Battles : Alma, Sept. 20, '54 ; Inkerman, Nov. 5, '54 ; Siege of Sebastopol, Oct., '54–Sept., '55.
        *d.* Results. Peace of Paris, March 30, '56.
            1. The Crimea restored to Russia.
            2. Russian claims in respect to Turkey withdrawn.

*C.* Alexander II., 1855–'81.
    I.  The Turko-Russian War, '77 and '78.
        *a.* Causes.
            1. Insurrections against Turkish government in Herzegovina, Servia, Montenegro and Bulgaria.
            2. Intervention of Russia.
        *b.* Russian victories. Shipka Pass, Plevna, Kars.

    *c*. Results.   Peace of San Stefano, March 3, '78.

        Congress of Berlin, June 13–July 13, '78.

        1. Montenegro, Servia, and Roumania independent states.

        2. Bulgaria and East Roumelia semi-dependent on the Porte.

        3. Bosnia and Herzegovina ceded to Austria.

        4. Part of Thessaly and Epirus ceded to Greece.

        5. Batoum, Kars and Ardaghan ceded to Russia.

II.   Epoch of tentative reform, '60–'70.

    *a*. Abolition of serfdom, ukase of Feb. 19, '61.

    *b*. Reform in provincial administration.   The Zeinstvo.

    *c*. Judicial reforms.   Trial by jury.

    *d*. Limited freedom of the press.

III.   The Nihilist revolt.   *Herzen, Bakunin, Krapotkine.*

    *a*. The Pilgrimage to the People, '70–'75.

    *b*. Rigorous suppression, '75–'78.

      "A destroyed generation."

    *c*. Systematic terrorism, '78—

      Assassination of Alexander II., March 13, '81.

    *d*. Extraordinary measures of the government.

        1. Arbitrary and secret arrest.

        2. Preventative detention.

        3. Trial by court-martial.

        4. Harsh punishment of political offenders.

          Exile to Siberia.

*D*.  Contemporary problems.

   I.   The political problem.

     "Absolutism tempered by assassination."

  II.   The social problem.

     The persecution of the Jews.

  III.   The industrial problem.

    *a*. Exorbitant taxation of the peasants.

    *b*. Failure of crops, summer of '91.

    *c*. Famine and pestilence of '91 and '92.

References :—

   Ramband : History of Russia.

     II.   Chapters XI., XII., XIII., XIV., XV.

   Kelley : History of Russia.

     II.   Chapters LIII.-LXXII.     ,

   Lamartine : Histoire de la Russie.

     II.   Livres VIII., IX., X.

   Morfill : Story of Russia.

     Chapters X., XI., XIII.

Müller : Political History of Recent Times.
      253–270, Crimean War.
      505–576, Turkey and the Russo-Turkish War.
Murdock : Reconstruction of Europe.
    Chapters V., VI., VII., VIII., the Crimean War.
Fyffe : Modern Europe.
    I.    Chapter X., campaign of 1812.
    II.   Chapter IV., war of Grecian independence.
    III.  Chapter III., Crimean War.
    III.  Chapter VII., the Eastern Question.
Alison : Modern Europe, 1815–1852.
    III.  Chapter XIV., war of Grecian independence.
    IV.  Chapter XXVI., revolution in Poland.
Dilke : Present Position of European Politics.  Chapter III.
Wallace : Russia.
    Chapters IV., XX., XXVII., the church.
            VI., VII., VIII., IX., XXIX.–XXXII., the peasantry.
            XIII., XIV., the government.
            XI., XVII., burgesses and noblesse.
            XXVIII., the Crimean War.
            XXXIV., expansion of Russia.
Geddie : Russian Empire.
    Chapters I., VII., IX.
Gerebtzoff : Civilization in Russia.
    I.  Chapter V.
    II.  48–67 ; chapter XII.
Leroy, Beaulieu : L'Empire des Tsars et les Russes.
    I.  Book VII. and VIII., the peasants.
    II.  Book I., the commune.
       Book II., the government.
       Book VI., revolutionary agitation.
    III.  Book II., the church.
       Book III., the dissenters.
Gurowski : Russia as it is (1854).
Stepniak : Underground Russia.
Stepniak : The Russian Peasantry.
Stepniak : Russia under the Czars.
Kennan : Siberia and the Exile System.
    I.  Chapters VIII., X., XI., XIII., XIV.
    II.  pp. 495–509.
Persecution of the Jews in Russia (pamphlet issued by Russo-Jewish Committee).
Review of Reviews, January, 1892.
    The Czar and Russia of To-day.  (Stead.)

Nineteenth Century.

    31 : 1, the Horrors of Hunger.

North American Review.

    154 : 541, the Famine in Russia.

Tolstoi : War and Peace.

Tourgenieff : Fathers and Sons.

THE DECLARATION OF RIGHTS, issued by the National Assembly of France, Aug. 27, 1789.

The representatives of the French people, met in National Assembly, considering that ignorance, forgetfulness, or contempt for the rights of man are the sole causes of public misfortunes and of the corruption of governments, have resolved to set forth, in a solemn declaration, the natural, inalienable, and sacred rights of man, in order that this declaration constantly before all the members of the social body, may perpetually recall to them their rights and their duties, so that they may the more respect the acts of the legislative power and those of the executive power, by being able to compare them constantly with the aim of every political institution, so that the demands of citizens, founded henceforth on simple and incontestable principles, may tend always to the upholding of the Constitution and to the well-being of all.

Consequently, the National Assembly recognizes and declares, in the presence and under the auspices of the Supreme Being, the following rights of men and citizens.

ARTICLE 1. Men are born and remain free and with the same rights. Social distinctions can be founded only upon the common good.

ART. 2. The aim of every political association is the preservation of the natural and imprescriptible rights of man. These rights are liberty, property, security, and resistance to oppression.

ART. 3. The principle of all sovereignty rests essentially in the nation. No body, no individual, can exercise authority which does not emanate directly from it.

ART. 4. Liberty consists in being able to do whatever does not injure another. Thus the only limits to the natural rights of man are those which secure to the other members of society the enjoyment of the same rights. These limits can be determined only by the law.

ART. 5. The law has the right to forbid only those actions that are harmful to society. All that is not forbidden by law cannot be prevented, and no one can be forced to do what the law does not order.

ART. 6. The law is the expression of the public desire. All citizens have the right to assist, personally or by their representatives, at its formation. It must be the same for all, whether it protects or punishes. All citizens, being equal in its eyes, are equally eligible for all dignities, offices, and public positions, according to their ability, and with no distinction but that of their virtues and their talents.

ART. 7. No man can be accused, arrested, or detained except in cases determined by the law, and in accordance with the forms which it has prescribed. Those who incite, originate, execute, or cause to be executed, arbitrary orders, must be punished; but every citizen summoned or seized in the name of the law must obey instantly; he renders himself culpable by resistance.

ART. 8. The law must establish only those penalties strictly necessary, and no one can be punished except by a law established and promulgated before the offense, and legally applied.

ART. 9. As every man is considered innocent until he has been proved guilty, if it is judged indispensable to arrest him, all rigor beyond that which is necessary for his detention, must be severely reprimanded by the law.

ART. 10. No one can be molested for his opinions, even religious, provided that their manifestation does not disturb the public peace established by the law.

ART. 11. The free communication of thoughts and opinions is one of the most precious rights of man; every citizen can, therefore, speak, write, or print freely, except in replying with the abuse of this liberty in cases determined by the law.

ART. 12. The guaranty of the rights of men and citizens necessitates a public authority. This authority is, therefore, instituted for the advantage of all, and not for the particular good of those in whom it is vested.

ART. 13. For the maintenance of the public force, and for the expenses of administration, a general tax is indispensable; it must be equally shared by all the citizens, in proportion to their resources.

ART. 14. All the citizens have the right to state, personally or by their representatives, the necessity of the public tax, to consent to it freely, to levy it, and establish its quota, assessment, payment, and duration.

ART. 15. Society has the right to demand an account from every public agent, of his administration.

ART. 16. Every society, in which the guaranty of rights is not assured, nor the division of powers determined, has no constitution.

ART. 17. As property is an inviolable and sacred right, no one can be deprived of it, except when public necessity, legally stated, actually exacts it, on condition of a just and necessary indemnity.

THE CONSTITUTION issued by the National Convention of the French people, June 24, 1793.

## OF THE REPUBLIC.

1. The French Republic is one and indivisible.

## OF THE DIVISION OF THE PEOPLE.

2. The French people is, for the purpose of exercising its sovereignty, divided into primary assemblies by cantons.

3. For the purpose of administration and justice, it is divided into departments, districts, and municipalities.

## OF THE RIGHT OF CITIZENSHIP.

4. Every man born and living in France, of twenty-one years of age, and every alien who has attained the age of twenty-one, and has been domiciled in France one year, and lives from his labor, or has acquired property, or has adopted a child, or supports an aged man ; and, finally, every alien whom the Legislative Body has declared as one well deserving of the human race, are admitted to exercise the rights of a French citizen.

5. The right of exercising the rights of a citizen is lost : by naturalization in a foreign state ; by acceptance of functions or favors which do not proceed from a democratic government ; by condemnation to dishonorable or corporal punishments, until reinstated in civil rights.

6. The exercise of the rights of citizens is suspended : by indictment ; by a sentence *in contumaciam*, so long as this sentence has not been annulled.

## OF THE SOVEREIGNTY OF THE PEOPLE.

7. The sovereign people embraces all French citizens.

8. It chooses its deputies directly.

9. It delegates to electors the choice of administrators, of public arbitrators, criminal judges, and judges of cassation.

10. It deliberates on laws.

## OF THE PRIMARY ASSEMBLIES.

11. The primary assemblies are formed of the citizens who have resided six months in a canton.

12. They consist of at least 200 and no more than 600 citizens, called together for the purpose of voting.

13. They are organized after a president, secretaries, and collectors of votes have been appointed.

14. They have their own police.

15. No one is allowed to appear there with arms.

16. The elections are conducted either by secret or open voting, at the pleasure of each voter.

17. A primary meeting cannot prescribe a uniform mode of voting.

18. The collectors of votes note down the votes of those citizens who cannot write and yet prefer to vote by ballot.

19. The votes on laws are given by "Yes" and "No."

20. The vote of the primary assemblies is published in the following manner : The united citizens in the Primary Assembly at . . . . . numbering . . . . . votes, vote for, or vote against, by a majority of . . . . .

## OF THE NATIONAL REPRESENTATION.

21. Population is the only basis of national representation.

22. For every 40,000 individuals one deputy is chosen.

23. Every primary assembly, which is formed of from 39,000 to 41,000 individuals, chooses directly a deputy.

24. The choice is effected by an absolute majority of votes.

25. Every assembly makes an abstract of the votes, and sends a commissioner to the appointed central place of general record.

26. If, at the first voting, no absolute majority be effected, a second meeting shall be held, and those two citizens who had the most votes shall be voted for again.

27. In case of an equal division of votes, the oldest person has the preference, either in selecting the person to be voted for, or to decide if he be elected. In case of an equality of age, the casting of lots shall decide.

28. Every Frenchman who enjoys the rights of a citizen is eligible throughout the whole Republic.

29. Every deputy belongs to the whole nation.

30. In case of nonacceptance, of resignation, or forfeiture of office, or of the death of a deputy, the primary assembly which had chosen him shall choose a person to fill the vacancy.

31. A deputy who tenders his resignation cannot leave his post until his successor shall have been appointed.

32. The French people assembles every year on the 1st of May to take part in the elections.

33. It proceeds thereto whatever the number of citizens present may be who have a right to vote.

34. Extraordinary primary meetings are held at the demand of one fifth of the eligible citizens.

35. The meeting is, in this case, called by the municipal authority at the usual place of assembly.

36. These extraordinary meetings can transact business only when at least more than one half of the qualified voters are present.

## OF THE ELECTORAL ASSEMBLIES.

37. The citizens united in primary assemblies nominate one elector in proportion to 200 citizens (present or not) ; two for from 301 to 600.

38. The holding of electoral assemblies and the mode of elections are the same as in the primary assemblies.

## OF THE LEGISLATIVE BODY.

39. The Legislative Body is one, indivisible and continual.

40. Its session lasts one year.

41. It assembles on the 1st of July.

42. The National Assembly cannot be organized unless at least one more than one half of the deputies are present.

43. The deputies can at no time be held answerable, accused, or condemned on account of opinions uttered within the Legislative Body.

44. In criminal cases, they may be arrested if taken in the act ; but the warrant of arrest and the warrant of committal can be issued only by the authority of the Legislative Body.

## MODE OF PROCEDURE OF THE LEGISLATIVE BODY.

45. The sessions of the National Assembly are public.

46. The minutes of their sessions shall be printed.

47. It cannot deliberate unless it consist of at least 200 members.

48. It cannot refuse the floor to members in the order in which they demand the same.

49. It decides by a majority of those present.

50. Fifty members have the right to demand a call by names.

51. It has the right of censorship on the conduct of its members.

52. It exercises the power of police at the place of its sessions, and within a certain jurisdiction it has determined.

## OF THE FUNCTIONS OF THE LEGISLATIVE BODY.

53. The Legislative Body proposes laws and issues decrees.

54. By the general name of law are understood the provisions of the Legislative Body which concern the civil and penal legislation ; the general administration of the revenues of the Republic ; the national domains ; the inscription, alloy, stamp, and names of coins ; the nature, the raising, and the collection of taxes ; declaration of war ; every new general division of the French territory ; public instruction ; public demonstrations of honor to the memory of great men.

55. By the particular name of decrees are understood those enactments of the Legislative Body which concern : the annual establishment of the land and marine forces ; the permission for or refusal of the marching of foreign troops through French territory ; the admission of foreign vessels of war into the ports of the Republic ; the measures for the general peace and safety ; the distribution of annual and momentary relief, and of public works ; the orders for the coining of moneys of every description ; the unforeseen and extraordinary expenses ; the local and particular measures for an administration, a commune, or any kind of public works ; the defense of the territory ; the ratification of treaties ; the nomination and dismissal of the commanders-in-chief of the armies ; the carrying into effect the responsibility of members of the Council, and of public officers ; the accusation of discovered conspiracies against the common safety of the Republic ; every alteration in the division of the French territory, and the national rewards.

#### OF THE MAKING OF LAWS.

56. A report must precede the introduction of a bill.

57. Not until after a fortnight from the report can the debate begin and the law be provisionally enacted.

58. The proposed law is printed and sent to all the communes of the Republic, entitled PROPOSED LAW.

59. If forty days after the sending in of the proposed law, an absolute majority of the departments, and one tenth of all the primary assemblies of each department, legally assembled, have not protested, the bill is accepted and becomes a law.

60. If protest be made, the Legislative Body calls together the primary assemblies.

#### ON THE SUPERSCRIPTION OF LAWS AND DECREES.

61. The laws, decrees, sentences, and all public acts are superscribed in the name of the French people, in the ——— year of the French Republic.

#### OF THE EXECUTIVE COUNCIL.

62. There shall be an Executive Council, consisting of twenty-four members.

63. The electoral assembly of each department nominates a candidate. The Legislative Body chooses the members of the Executive Council from this general list.

64. It shall be renewed each half session of every legislature, in the last months of its session.

65. The Executive Council is charged with the management and supervision of the general administration. Its activity is limited to the execution of laws and decrees of the Legislative Body.

66. It appoints, outside of its own body, the highest agents of the general administration of the Republic.

67. The Legislative body establishes the number and the business of these agents.

68. These agents do not form a council. They are separated one from the other, and have no relation with each other. They exercise no personal power.

69. The Executive Council chooses, outside of its own body, the foreign agents of the Republic.

70. It negotiates treaties.

71. The members of the Executive Council are, in case of violation of duties, accused by the Legislative Body.

72. The Executive Council is responsible for the nonexecution of the laws and decrees, and the abuses of which it does not give notice.

73. It recalls and substitutes the agents at pleasure.

74. It is obliged, if there is cause, to inform the judicial authorities regarding them.

## OF THE MUTUAL RELATIONS BETWEEN THE EXECUTIVE COUNCIL AND THE LEGISLATIVE BODY.

75. The Executive Council shall have its seat near the Legislative Body ; shall have admittance to, and a special seat at, the place of session.

76. It shall be heard at all times when it shall have a statement to make.

77. The Legislative Body shall call the Council before it, in whole or in part, when it is thought necessary.

### OF THE ADMINISTRATIVE AND MUNICIPAL BODIES.

78. There shall be a municipal administration in each commune of the Republic, and in each district an intermediate administration, and in each department a central administration.

79. The municipal officers are chosen by the assemblies of the commune.

80. The administrators are chosen by the electoral assemblies of the departments and of the districts.

81. The municipalities and the administrations are annually renewed one half.

82. The administrators, authorities, and municipal officers have not a representative character. They can, in no case, modify the acts of the Legislative Body, nor suspend the execution of them.

83. The Legislative Body assigns the business of the municipal officers and of the administrators, the rules regarding their subordination, and the punishments to which they may become liable.

84. The sessions of the municipalities and of the administrations are public.

85. The civil and penal code is the same for the whole Republic.

86. No encroachment can be made upon the right of citizens to have their matters in dispute decided on by arbitrators of their own choice.

87. The decision of these arbitrators is final, unless the citizens have reserved the right of protesting.

88. There shall be justices of the peace, chosen by the citizens of the districts, according to law.

89. They shall arbitrate and hold court without fees.

90. Their number and jurisdiction shall be established by the Legislative Body.

91. There shall be public judges of arbitration, who are chosen by electoral assemblies.

92. Their number and districts are fixed by the Legislative Body.

93. They shall decide on matters in controversy which have not been brought to a final decision by private arbitrators or by the justices of the peace.

94. They shall deliberate publicly. They shall vote orally. They decide in the last resort on oral pleadings, or on a simple petition, without legal forms and without costs. They shall assign the reasons of their decisions.

95. The justices of the peace and the public arbitrators are chosen annually.

96. In criminal cases, no citizen can be put on trial, except a true bill of complaint be found by a jury, or by the Legislative Body.

The accused shall have advocates, either chosen by themselves or appointed officially.

The proceedings are in public.

The facts and the intention are passed upon by a jury.

The punishment is executed by a criminal tribunal.

97. The criminal judges are chosen annually by the electoral assemblies.

98. There is a Court of Cassation for the whole Republic.

99. This court takes no cognizance of the facts. It decides on the violation of matters of form, and on questions of law.

100. The members of this court are appointed annually by the electoral assemblies.

#### OF THE GENERAL TAXES.

101. No citizen is excluded from the honorable obligation to contribute toward the public expenses.

#### OF THE NATIONAL TREASURY.

102. The national treasury is the central point of the revenues and expenses of the Republic.

103. It is managed by responsible agents, whom the Executive Council shall elect.

104. These agents are supervised by commissioners, whom the Legislative Body shall appoint, but who cannot be taken from their own body; they are responsible for abuses of which they do not give legal notice.

#### OF THE RENDITION OF ACCOUNTS.

105. The accounts of the agents of the national treasury, and those of the administrators of public moneys are rendered annually to responsible commissioners appointed by the Executive Council.

106. Those persons appointed to revise the accounts are supervised by the commissioners, who are elected by the Legislative Body, not out of their own number; and they are responsible for the frauds and mistakes of accounts of which they do not give notice.

The Legislative Body passes upon the accounts.

#### OF THE MILITARY FORCES OF THE REPUBLIC.

107. The general military force of the Republic consists of the whole people.

108. The Republic supports, also, in time of peace, a paid land and marine force.

109. All Frenchmen are soldiers; all shall be exercised in the use of arms.

110. There is no generalissimo.

111. The distinction of grade, the military marks of distinction and subordination, exist only in service and for the time of its duration.

112. The public force employed to maintain order and peace in the interior acts only on a written requisition of the constituted authorities.

113. The public force employed against foreign enemies is under the command of the Executive Council.

114. No armed body can deliberate.

#### OF THE NATIONAL CONVENTION.

115. If the absolute majority of departments and the tenth part of their regularly formed primary assemblies demand a revision of the Constitution, or an alteration of some of its articles, the Legislative Body is

compelled to call together all primary assemblies of the Republic, in order to ascertain whether a National Convention shall be called.

116. The National Convention is formed in like manner as the legislatures, and unites in itself the highest power.

117. It is occupied, as regards the Constitution, only with those subjects which caused it to be called together.

#### OF THE RELATIONS OF THE FRENCH REPUBLIC TOWARD FOREIGN NATIONS.

118. The French nation is the natural friend and ally of free nations.

119. It does not interfere with the affairs of government of other nations. It suffers no interference of other nations with its own.

120. It offers an asylum for all who, on account of liberty, are banished from their native country. These it refuses to deliver up to tyrants.

121. It concludes no peace with an enemy that holds possession of its territory.

#### OF THE GUARANTY OF RIGHTS.

122. The Constitution guarantees to all Frenchmen equality, liberty, security, property, the public debt, free exercise of religion, general instruction, public assistance, absolute liberty of the press, the right of petition, the right to hold popular assemblies, and the enjoyment of all the rights of man.

123. The French Republic respects loyalty, courage, old age, filial affection, misfortune. It places the Constitution under the guarantee of all virtues.

124. The declaration of the rights of man and the Constitutional Act shall be engraven on tables, to be placed in the midst of the Legislative Body, and in public places.